THEMED-JOKES

&

RIDDLES

183

Sometimes, what we're looking for is right in front of us, hidden in plain sight and the answer is simpler than we think, hidden in the code of the question itself.

Contents

Riddles

1) What comes once in a minute, twice in a moment, but never in a thousand years?

The answer is the letter "M." It appears once in the word "minute," twice in the word "moment," but not at all in the phrase "a thousand years."

**2) The more you take, the more you leave behind.
what am I?**

The answer is "footsteps." when you take more footsteps, you leave behind more footprints.

3) The person who makes it, sells it. The person who buys it never uses it. The person who uses it never know they're using it.

The answer is "a coffin."

4) I speak without a mouth and hear without ears. I have nobody, but I come alive with the wind. What am I?

The answer is an "echo." An echo speaks without a mouth, hears without ears, and
comes alive with the wind.

5) What has keys but can't open locks?

The answer is a "piano." A piano has keys but
can't open locks.

**6) What has cities but no houses, forests but no
trees, and rivers but no water?**

The answer is a "map." A map has cities, forests,
and rivers, but it doesn't contain
actual houses, trees, or water.

7) What is always in front of you but can't be seen?

The answer is the future. The future is always in front of you, but you can't see it.

8) I'm not alive, but I can grow. I don't have lungs, but I need air. I don't have a mouth, but water kills me. What am I?

The answer is "a flame or a fire"

9) I may seem real, but it always turns out. I was never there in the first place... You only see me during a certain resting stage. What am I?

The answer is "a dream."

**10) You see me once in June, twice in November, but not at all in May.
What am I?**

The answer is the letter "M."

**11) I am the beginning of the end, and the end of time and space. I am essential to creation, and I surround every place.
What am I?**

The answer is the letter "e." It's the beginning of "end," the end of "time" and "space," present in "creation," and indeed, it surrounds many places.

**12) I am always hungry, I must always be fed. The finger I touch will soon turn red.
What am I?**

The answer is "fire." Fire is always hungry for fuel, it must always be fed to keep burning.

**13) I am taken from a mine and shut up in a wooden case, from which I am never released, and yet I am used by almost every person.
What am I?"**

The answer is "a pencil lead." A pencil is taken from a mine (graphite mine), encased in wood, and used by almost every person.

**14) I am full of holes, but I can still hold water.
What am I?"**

The answer is "a sponge." A sponge is full of holes but can still hold water due to its absorbent nature.

**15) I have keys, but no locks and space, but no room. You can enter, but can't go outside.
What am I?**

The answer is "keyboard."

16) I have no life, but I can die. I have no mouth, but I can speak. I have no limbs, but I can move. What am I?

The answer is "a battery." A battery has no life, but it can die. It has no mouth, but it can speak.
It has no limbs, but it can move.

17) I have a face, but no eyes. I have hands, but no fingers. I have no mouth, but I can tell you something. What am I?

The answer is a watch. A watch has a face, but no eyes. It has hands, but no fingers. It has no
mouth, but it can tell you something.

18) I have a head and a tail, but no body. I can be flipped, but I'm not a pancake. I can be spent, but I'm not a dollar. What am I?

The answer is "a coin" A coin has a head and a tail, but no body. It can be flipped, but it's not a pancake. It can be spent, but it's not a dollar.

**19) I have a tongue, but no mouth. I have a soul, but no body. I can be worn, but I'm not clothes.
What am I?**

The answer is a shoe. A shoe has a tongue, but no mouth. It has a soul, but no body. It can be worn, but it's not clothes.

**20) I have a voice, but no mouth. I have words, but no letters. I have a language, but no grammar.
What am I?**

The answer is "a song." A song has a voice, but no mouth. It has words, but no letters. It has a language, but no grammar.

21) I have a face, but no expression. I have hands, but no touch. I have numbers, but no math. What am I?

The answer is "a clock." A clock has a face, but no expression. A clock has hands, but no touch.
A clock has numbers, but no math.

22) The more of this there is, the less you see. What is it?

The answer is "darkness." The more darkness there is, the less you can see.

23) I fly without wings, I cry without eyes. Whenever I go, darkness flies. What am I?

The answer is "clouds." Clouds can "fly" across the sky without wings, and they can "cry" by raining, even though they don't have eyes

24) What goes up but never comes down?

The answer is "age."

Themed Jokes

25) what do you get if you cross a snowman and a dog?

The answer is "frostbite."

26) What do you call a cat on the beach during Christmas time?

The answer is "Sandy claws!"

27) What do you call an elf who sings?

The answer is "a wrapper"

28) What do you call Santa when he takes a break?

The answer is 'Santa pause"

29) what do you call a snowman with a six-pack?

The answer is "an abdominal snowman"

30) Why did the computer go to the doctor?

Because it had a virus!

31) Why was the math book sad?

Because it had too many problems!

32) Why did the scarecrow win an award?

Because he was outstanding in his field!

33) Why did the tomato turn red?

Because it saw the salad dressing!

34) Why don't scientists trust atoms?

Because they make up everything!

35) Why did the photon bring a suitcase to the airport?

Because it was traveling light!

36) Why don't skeletons fight each other?

Because they don't have the guts!

37) Why couldn't the bicycle stand up by itself?

Because it was two tired!

38) What do you call a fish wearing a crown?

A kingfish!

39) Why do bees have sticky hair?

Because they use honeycombs!

40) What did one wall say to the other wall?

I'll meet you at the corner!

41) Why did the scarecrow win an award?

Because he was outstanding in his field.

42) Why did the golfer bring two pairs of pants?

In case he got a hole in one!

43) What do you call a snake that works for the government?

A civil serpent!

44) What do you get when you cross a math teacher and a vampire?

Count Dracula!

45) Why couldn't the leopard play hide and seek?

Because he was always spotted!

46) How does a penguin build it's house?

Igloos it together!

47) Want to hear a construction joke?

Oh, never mind, I'm still working on that one!

48) Why did the student eat his homework?

Because the teacher told him it was a piece of cake!

49) Why did the teacher wear sunglasses to school?

Because her students were so bright!

50) Why did the student do multiplication problems on the floor?

The teacher told him not to use tables!

51) What do you call a fish that wears a bowtie?

Sofishticated!

52) How do you get straight A's in school?

By using a ruler!

53) I told my wife she should embrace her mistakes.

She hugged me!

54) What do you call an internet page dedicated to anime?

A weebsite!

55) What's a boxer's favorite drink?

Fruit punch!

56) What's the hardest thing in skateboarding?

The concrete!

57) What did the baby robot call its creator?

Da-ta!

Food-themed Jokes

58) What do you call fake spaghetti?

An impasta!

59) Why did the cookie go to the doctor?

Because it was feeling crumbly!

60) What do you call cheese that is not yours?

Nacho cheese

61) What do you call a bear that likes to eat honey?

A Winnie-the-Pooh bear!

62) What do you call a potato that has turned to the dark side?

A Vader tot!

63) What do you call a boomerang that doesn't come back?

A stick of butter!

64) What do you call a melon that's not allowed to get married?

A cantaloupe!

65) How do you organize a space party?

You planet!

66) Why did the coffee file a police report?

Because it got mugged!

67) Why did the banana go to the doctor?

Because it wasn't peeling well!

68) Why did the mushroom go to the party?

Because he's a fungi!

69) Why did the lettuce win the race?

Because it was a "head" of the competition!

Sports-theme Jokes

70) Why did the football coach go to the bank?

To get his quarterback!

71) Why do basketball players love cookies?

Because they can dunk them!

72) Why was the football field hot after the game?

Because all the fans left!

73) Why did the chicken join the soccer team?

Because it heard the coach was a great egg-spert.

74) How do you make a water polo player laugh?

By telling a pool joke.

75) What do you call an insect that's good at baseball?

A cricket!

76) Why did the basketball team go to the bank?

Because they wanted to get a new "shooting guard"!

77) Why don't fish play basketball?

Because they are afraid of the net!

78) How does a tennis player stay cool?

They stand near the fans!

**79) What did one tennis ball say
to the other tennis ball?**

"See you round the court!"

**80) Why do tennis players
always carry a pen?**

In case they need to draw a deuce!

**81) Why was the tennis club's
website down?**

Because they had problems with
their server!

82) Why do volleyball players love to visit the bakery?

Because they always enjoy a good serve!

83) Why do volleyball players make good secret agents?

Because they are experts at setting up covert operations!

84) Why was the volleyball player so good at math?

Because they knew how to "serve" up some great calculations!

85) Why did the soccer player bring string to the game?

So they could tie the score!

86) Why are soccer players excellent at math?

Because they know how to use their heads to score goals!

87) Why do soccer players do well in school?

Because they know how to use their headers!

Tech-themed Jokes

88) How do you get in touch with an android?

You have to use a CELL Phone!

89) What do you call a Japanese cartoon about old ladies?

A Granimae!

90) What do you call a computer that sings?

A Dell!

91) Why was the computer cold?

Because it left its Windows open!

92) Why do programmers prefer dark mode?

Because the light attracts bugs!

93) How does a computer get drunk?

It takes screenshots!

94) Why did the computer keep its drinks on the motherboard?

Because it was good at multitasking!

95) Why did the computer keep it's drinks on the mouse pad?

Because it was afraid of spilling it's Java!

96) Did you hear about the computer that fell out of the window?

It had a hard drive!

97) Why was the cell phone wearing glasses?

Because it lost all its contacts!

98) How many programmers does it take to change a light bulb?

None, that's a hardware problem!

99) Why did the programmer quit his job?

Because he didn't get arrays!

100) What do you get when you cross a computer and a lifeguard?

A screensaver!

101) How do you keep a programmer in the shower all day?

Give him a bottle of shampoo that says "lather, rinse, repeat!

102) Why did the computer go to therapy?

Because it had too many unresolved issues and couldn't handle its cache of problems!

103) Why don't programmers like nature?

Because ut has too many bugs.

104) What happens when a hard drive gets into a fight?

It asks for a back-up!

105) Why were the horses struggling to use the internet?

Because they were not able to find any stable connections.

Anime-themed Jokes

106) Why don't anime characters ever get lost?

Because they always follow their Naruto-vigation system!

107) Why did the anime fan bring a ladder to the bar?

Because they heard the drinks were on the house!

108) Why did the anime character go to the doctor?

To get a 'check-up' on their health points!

109) Why did the Gundam pilot get a parking ticket?

Because he was mecha-nically parked in a no-robot zone!

110) How do you know if someone's been watching too much Attack on Titan?

They start doing all their shopping at Wall-mart!

111) Why do anime characters always look good in photos?

Because they have "animézing" filters!

112) Why did the anime character go to school?

To improve his drawing skills!

113) Why did the anime character break up with their calculator?

Because it couldn't count on them!

114) Why did the anime character bring a pencil to the party?

In case they needed to draw some attention!

115) Why was the anime character always calm during battle?
Because they had 'zen' mode activated!

116) Why did the anime character always carry a map?

Because they kept getting lost in all those filler episodes!

117) Why did the anime character always carry a pencil?
In case they needed to draw their weapon!

118) Why did the anime character start a gardening club at school?

Because they heard it was a great way to "grow" as a person!

119) Why did the anime character bring a ladder to the library?

Because they heard the book they wanted was on the top shelf of the manga section!

120) Why did the anime character go to school in the summer?

To get ahead in class!

121) Why did the anime character bring a pillow to the fight?

To ensure they had a "soft landing" after defeating their opponents!

122) Why did the anime character always carry a mirror?

Because they wanted to reflect on their inner strength before every battle!

123) How do you get a date with an anime character?

You have to be on their wavelength.

124) What do you call an internet page dedicated to anime?

A weebsite.

125) Why did the anime character go to the dentist?

To get a better "bite."

126) Why did the anime character go to the computer store?

To get a better resolution in life!

127) Why do anime characters never go broke?

Because they always have a lot of yen!

128) What do you call an anime character with a cold?

A-sneezy!

129) Why did the anime character go to school with a sword?

Because they heard it was a cutting-edge institution!

Animal-themed Jokes

130) What do you get when you cross a sheep and a kangaroo?

A woolly jumper!

131) What do you call a bear that has no teeth?

A gummy bear!

132) What do you call a dog that can tell time?

A watch dog!

133) What do you call a cow that has a sense of humor?

A punny cow!

134) Why don't elephants use computers?

Because they're afraid of the mouse!

135) How do you catch a squirrel?

Climb a tree and act like a nut!

**136) Why did the cow go to outer
space?**

To see the moooon!

**137) Why don't seagulls fly over
the bay?**

Because then they would be
bagels!

**138) What do you call a group of
musical whales?**

An orca-stra!

139) Why did the crab never share his food?

Because he was a little shellfish!

140) What do you call a pile of cats?

A meowtain!

141) Why did the spider go to the computer?

To check his website!

142) Why did the bee get married?

Because he found his honey!

143) What do you call a fly without wings?

A walk!

144) Why did the ant refuse to come to the picnic?

Because it was already full!

145) Why did the fly never land on the computer?

Because it was afraid of the world wide web!

166) What do you call a bee that can't make up it's mind?

A maybe!

147) What did the mommy bee say to the naughty baby bee?

Bee-hive yourself!

148) Why did the firefly always forget the words to the song?

Because it wasn't very bright!

149) What did the bee say to the flower?

Hello, honey!

150) What do you call a bee that's having a bad hair day?

A frisbee!

151) What is a mosquito's favorite sport?

Skin diving!

152) Why did the ant refuse to share its food?

Because it was **ant**-social!

153) Why did the spider break up with the fly?

Because it found someone more **web-savvy**!

154) Why do zebras never get lost?

Because even if they're in a black-and-white world, they always stick to the stripes!

155) What did the zebra say when it saw a piano?

"I'm going to play in black and white keys!"

156) What do you call a group of zebras playing music?

A "black and white" band!

Zombie-themed Jokes

157) Why don't zombies like fast food?

Because they can't catch it!

158) Why did the zombie go to school?

To improve his "dead"-ucation!

159) Why do zombies make terrible comedians?

Because their jokes are always rotten!

160) Why did the zombie break up with his girlfriend?

Because she said he was too "dead" inside!

161) Why did the zombie go to the party alone?

He couldn't find a body to go with!

162) How do zombies keep their hair in place?

With scare-spray!

163) What do you call a zombie who tells good jokes?

A "dead" comedian!

164) Why don't zombies eat clowns?

Because they taste funny!

165) Why did the zombie go to the party?

Because he wanted to have a **grave** time!

166) How does a zombie greet you?

It says "Nice to eat you!"

167) If the Joker actor was the only zombie in a web series what would it be called?

The Joaquin Dead!

168) What is a zombie sleepover called?

Mass grave!

169) Why did the zombie go to therapy?

Because he was feeling a bit...dead inside!

170) Why did the zombie start a garden?

Because he wanted to grow some fresh brains!

171) What do zombies say before a fight?

"Do you want a piece of me?"

**172) Why did the zombie refuse
to fight the skeleton?**

He didn't have the stomach for it!

**173) What's a zombie's favorite
street to hunt?**

A dead-end street!

**174) Why did the zombie ignore
all his new emails?**

Because he was too busy looking
for the living attachments!

175) Why was the zombie always losing his debates?

Because he couldn't form a coherent head-argument!

176) How do zombies keep their breath fresh?

They use "tomb"paste!

177) What's a zombie's favorite shampoo?

Head & Shoulders!

178) What do you call a zombie who wins an award?

The "dead" of the class!

179) What do you get when you cross a zombie and a puppy?

A "dead" loyal companion!

180) What do you call a zombie who tells lies?

A "rotten" scoundrel!

181) What did the zombie say to his date?

"Are you dead-tired? Because you've been running through my mind all night!"

182) What do you call a zombie who likes to dance?

A thriller!

183) What do you call a flesh eating bee?

A zombee!